THE CAMPUS OF GOD'S WORD

The fact is that anyone born into this world is a student, regardless of your age, tribe, religion, or language you are a student before the Holy Spirit. In as much as you occupied a space in this world, you are a student. Every day we learn new things, each day we come in contact with new people either in the school, market, or in our working place, or our worship centers. And by I t, we upgrade our knowledge and expand our vision in life. God has employed a teacher who will teach you all that you need to know concerning yourself, your environment and the earth at large, John14:26:"But the Comforter, which is the Holy Spirit, whom the Father will send in my name, he shall teach you all thing, and bring all things to your remembrance, …". So we're meant to be productive and not tossed out because we have a good teacher. We are the reason for the creation. We are meant to legislate the order of things in our lives because he has given us the power to rule. He has put us in charge of the whole earth. Genesis 1:26, "And God said, let us make man in our image, after our likeness: and let them have dominion over the fish of the sea, and over the fowl of the air, and over the cattle, and over all the earth, and over every creeping thing that creped upon the earth". So there shall not be anyone poor among you. If you can rule your life with such mentality that you have all it takes to succeed and that you are created for purpose; you are at the top like the Eagle. John the Evangelist understood everything about spiritual wealth, success, and prosperity and physical wealth, success, and prosperity. He knew that spiritual success is of no use for a man until is being made physical. Wealth, success, and prosperity are not meant to be spiritual alone, but they should also be seen physically. John the Evangelist said, "Beloved, I wish above all things that you. may prosper and be in health, even as your soul prospers. In this book, you will learn something beneficial to yourself and your family, and your environment, but hear this. The enormous deficit we own ourselves in linearity with existence, nature, and humanity is to do the right thing at the right time, and that's what gives life meaning. The major contract the Father has committed into our hands is to spread abroad his word, and that's the way we can maximize wealth dividends. The Lord God by his creative nature shows us the right way to propagate riches and blessings and what we should do to live a life of joy overflowing. The reason why God started creating things or making things real is this: he never accepts blank space, he loved filling blank space with potential contents, he hates emptiness sand darkness, he has a man in his heart; he loves man so much that he could not put the man whom he had made in formless s and void earth. That's why he began his work when he saw that the earth is formless and void_ man was God's aim of creation. Prosperity, wealth, success, riches, good health, wellbeing, breakthrough, and financial speed are all good for man, and God allows it to exist just for man 'swell-being. God demonstrated the incredible power of his reality by bringing things into existence. The Son (Jesus Christ) had shown us the possibility of divine supply by feeding five thousand men though the women were not counted nor the children numbered. He taught us how to dwell our hearts and our minds on the campus of God's word_ surrounding ourselves with God's Word. Believing in his mighty works around your surroundings gives you a greater advantage to make an exploit in your world. The campus of God's word as we may say talks about the field, Land space, or premises in which you can build your heart, hope, faith, and confidence. The earth is like an estate well-built and designed with numerous rooms; each room has its padlock; each room is accessible to those who have the right keys. There are extensive blessings of things to survive with here on earth, but it can be accessible by those who have the right keys and those who know what to do. Until you change what you are doing, you can't have a different result. God is a spirit-filled with power and might but when he needed something to transpire into the physical realm he made a move that gave rise to creation. The Bible has it that God saw that it was very good and they were all good (Genesis 1:31). So he spoke what he wanted and it came to pass as he had desired. That means that we are connected to the realm through what we say. Your ability to understand the power of God's Word is the higher your achievement is because God's Word is the fundamental key that grants you to fly above all phases of life like the Eagle flying to the country of its Destination. Each student who makes his abode on the campus has the aim of graduating one day. In the standard of education, a graduate student is seen as a perfect student regarding his/her field of study. In the campus of God's Word, the Teacher had said, "Be ye therefore perfect, even as your Father which is in heaven is perfect ", (Matthew 5:48, KJV). Now, hear this, we are created by God in his image and likeness, as he is so being we here on earth. God is perfect, and we're perfect because he made us. But today, man has lost his perfection; that's why he has sent his Holy Spirit to re-perfect us again. So, as we dwell in this Campus, (earth) we are to be taught by the Lecturer (the Holy Spirit) so that we can meet up with the standard of God our maker. This book is aimed at dropping down some keys that will help you to propagate wealth dividends. The Creator of humanity made to himself available all the elements He needed for the making of man because man was his primary purpose of creating things. Furthermore, for Him to accomplish his project, He called upon other heavenly contractors (the Son and the Holy Spirit) to come alongside to ensure perfection during the making of the man (Genesis 1:26). Thereafter, God saw all that He had created and he found no error in them because they are well made. He saw that all He did was nice He made all things perfect and they were good. In (Matthew 5:48) Jesus instructed us to be perfect in wisdom, knowledge, and understanding so that we can maintain well-being and unlimited access to good things of life. He wants us to have a mature heart. That's to say even though we abode on the campus of his words, we ought to live with perfect hearts and minds. That means that Our reasoning for existing ought to be reasonablebecausewearemadeperfectandwehaveaperfectteacher(HolyGhost). We are the students of God's word, His perfect Spirit is our orator (John 14:26), "...He shall teach you all things and bring all things to your remembrance...". As students we are, the Campus owner expected us to be humble and obedient to His instructions so that we can be well taught. As students we are, our upgrade is in his hands; We can't afford anything and we have nothing except what is being given to us from above. God being the Head of all things, wants us to know the importance of his word in our lives. Just as food is important for us to eat and live, He wants us to be fed with his word; and live with the consciousness that nothing else could be good for us if we could not abide permanentlyInthespokenwordofhismouth_that'sthebeginningofoursuccess. Matthew 4:4 said, &But he answered and said, it is written, man shall not live by bread alone, but by every word that proceeded out of the mouth of God &. Regarding where we read, we understand that the speaker did not take away bread from us; but he let us understand that while we ate bread, we should also have in us the words that came out of God's mouth. Now hear this, most believers thought that prosperity is a sin, no! No! No! Hundred times No! Prosperity is one of the things God adds to a man for well-being. Prosperity is a decorative material around a man. God used prosperity to nurture the living aspects of a man. Just as food is important to our body so prosperity is important to man. That was why when God saw that the earth was poor, he desired to make the earth rich because he hates poverty as a man hates a lack of food. It is recommendable to know that a consistent food supply is what gives energy, Power, stability, and strength to the body. The Bible recorded that Elijah the Prophet went in the strength of food for forty days and forty nights. 1king 19 :8: And he arose, and did eat and drink, and went in the strength of that meat(food) for forty days and forty nights, unto Horeb the mount of GOD. Food is a "body blow amplifier "it makes the body boastful and healthy. And that's what gives life to the body of a man. Every believer needs to be invariably fed with God's Word. Newborn babies are fed with the constant milk supply from breastfeeding mothers. This talk about those mommies who give suck to their Little ones. Research has shown that constant natural supply from the origin of creation is what keeps the earth moving; as food is essential to our growth and physical fitness likewise is essential to us the believers to mass our lives and our whole heart on the campus of God's Word. We exist in God's word because the earth that we are living today came into being through the spoken word of his mouth. The spoken word of His mouth had brought things into being, and we're the reason for creation. Sincerely, God loves man. The earth is the Campus assembled by His Word. Through Him, all things above and beneath the surface of the earth were made. Conception, it is the will of God that each of His sons and daughters should live with an unlimited supply of words that He had spoken to us because that's the key to prosperity. Joshua 1v8 KJV. The Bible said, "this book of the law shall not evacuate out of thy mouth, but thou shalt meditate therein day and night, that thou Mayes observe to do according to all that is written therein: then thou shalt make thy ways prosperous and then thou shalt have success". The Gospel truth is that it is the blessing attached to the word of the Lord that makes a man rich, not much struggle or hard labor that makes a man rich. Hard work gives you more room to think about when you intend to have success through hard labor. We are not created to struggle but to enjoy his riches in glory. You will have many complicated issues to solve before you can obtain riches through hard labor. But when God gives you, He filters out sorrows and embarrassment and makes things easier for you. In the Bible, the Psalmist gave us a clear picture of what our lives ought to be when we inhabit our minds on the campus of God's Word and that gave us a magnificent image of how glorious it is when we commit ourselves to the word of the Lord. Psalm 1:2: But his delight is in the law of the Lord, and in his law does he meditate days and nights. Now move to verse 3: "And he shall be like a tree planted by the rivers of water, that brings fourth his fruit in his season; his leaf also shall not wither, and what so ever he doeth shall prosper". Let's give little attention to this: when you ponder your mind in the words of the Lord, and you stick to it, you capitalize on it, that's you live by it day and night. When you cogitate fully over and over again, you automatically receive a constant heat supply that vitalizes your soul and gives you room for well-being. And that will equally give you more life to your soul and things around you. Not just vitalizing your soul, but reflecting on the areas of your life e.g. business, marriage, academics, job, and many other significant areas of your life. Using hand made of God's work, let's take a good example of these two classes of living things. Mammals and Birds; and other sets of animals that are not in the same class as mammals. Mammals and birds are homoeothermic; all other animals are poikilothermic. A homoiotherm* (Greek: homoios, = constant; themes, = heat) is an animal that maintains a nearly constant body temperature, regardless of the changes in the temperature surrounding them, they maintain constant body temperature. A poikilotherm* (Greek: poi kilos, varied). This is an animal whose body temperature varies with the outside temperature. It rises in hot weather and falls in cold weather. Being homoeothermic gives birds and mammals a greater advantage over other animals. This means that they can be functional, active at all times, they are not limited to any weather condition. Now when a reptile such as a cobra, or lizard, for example, is either sluggish, or inactive because its body temperature is low, or has to rest in the shade to avoid becoming too warmed (poi kilos).

Mammals (homeotherms) for example, man or bird can hunt for food or actively stay away from an enemy, they can operate under a high sun density. Regardless of weather conditions, man operates under cold weather and hot weather all the time. At times when other animals are inactive, man, lion, or bird are active. For instance, the feathers of a bird are never undermined to fly, the paw of a lion is ever active to function, the horn of a cow is never pulled out of its head. And man's legs are not weak except for old age. They are functional at all times. In other words, the homeothermic (birds and mammals), have to eat more than other animals to provide the energy, stability, power, or strength needed to maintain constant body temperature. Likewise, the believers, God wants us to stay steamed at all times, and to be fed with his words, that we might be able to regulate, maintain a steady energy supply needed for us to grow our prosperous soul. We metamorphose our present conditions by absorbing more and more of God's Word and that gives room for well-being. Every mammal has a body regulator that enables them to maintain constant body temperature; that makes it possible for them to withstand all weather conditions. We all have a prosperous soul, YES! We know that. But not all of us are prospering in the physical. Yeah! Understand that mammals consume more food to retain constant heat and that enables them to govern their physical state. What should we do to enable our prosperous souls to reflect our physical state? Yeah! That's a good question to ask. In 3 John 1:2, the writer says, "Beloved, I wish above all things that thou Mayes prosper and be in good health, even as thy soul prospered". Now the writer wishes us physical prosperity, knowing well that it is possible to have a prosperous soul and not prospering in the physical state. He wished that our physical success should be Linear to our prosperous soul. And that be the mind of God for his people. Now for us to usher out the prosperity of the soul into our physical lives is not different from what Joshua said. Joshua 1:8, the Bible says, "This book of the law shall not depart out of thy mouth; but thou shalt meditate therein day and night, that thou Mayes observe to do according to all that is written therein: for then thou shalt make thy way prosperous, and then thou shalt have success". Now, let's get something from the places we read, in the 3rd book of John 1:2, the writer (John the Evangelist) when he was at Ephesus. He wished the people physical prosperity as their soul prospered. He did it when he found out that the people who are called by the Lord are prosperous in their souls and not in their physical state. This means that the prosperous attributes of your soul should also be seen in the physical aspects of your life. The Bible told us how to make it happen. In Joshua1:8, the writer(Joshua), open up to us how to make it happen; he said, "This book of the law shall not depart out of thy mouth; but thou shalt meditate therein day and night, that thou Mayes observe to do according to all that is written therein: for then thou shalt make thy way prosperous, and then thou shalt have success." Meditation is the gateway to success; it will supply your constant energy needful for your growth, both within you and outside you. In the book of Psalms 1:2,3, the author (the Psalmist) said something impressive, "But his delight is in the law of the Lord; and in his law does he meditate day and night". Let's proceed to V3 of the same chapter, "And he shall be like a tree planted by the rivers of water, that Brings forth his fruit in his season; his leaves also shall not wither, and what so ever he doeth shall prosper". Mammals conserve energy needed to maintain a healthy living, they eat more to retain constant body temperature. The author of Psalms accurately revealed the life of a man whose delight is in the laws of the Lord,2

"...that bring forth his fruit in his season, his leaf also shall not wither..." This means that they don't catch a cold easily in cool weather, they are not affected by some environmental factors. They are productive, they don't miss the period of their prosperity. These are those whose delight is in the law; they make abode within the "Campus of God's Word". In other words, they are not like poikilotherm. Poikilotherm* (Greek word: poikilos, = varied) is an animal whose temperature differs from the outside temperature. The word poikilotherm has two syllabi, the first one is & poikilos' 'which means varied. These are animals whose body temperature varies with the outside temperature. Its body temperature gets hot in hot weather and falls in cold weather. This set of animals are mostly influenced by the weather conditions of an environment. They hardly comprehend a higher or lower situation of an environment. In our today's English language, the terms 'coldblooded 'and 'warm-blooded' are commonly used instead of poikilothermic, = (reptiles e.g. lizards) and homeothermic, = (mammals e.g. man) being warm-blooded. Being warm-blooded enables mammals to have an advantage over the rest of the animals. It helps them to succeed in all areas of their lives. God's purpose of creation was for us to live and dominate the earth. God created all things and He made us the innkeeper of his invention. Man was a key reason for creation, all that is within the earth is for man's use, so it is righteousness for a man to live in the abundance of wealth and prosperity. Well-Being gives a man strength as food gives the body strength. Regarding human biology, consistent food gives stamina and makes the body strong. Newborns are periodically fed with the milk supply from the nursing mamas; Which enables them to thrive up. A Believer whose delight is in the words of the Lord shall thrive up, and shall not wither. Those who read and understand, absorb, and assimilate the words of the Lord are those who brings forth fruit in their seasons.

Such people are known as 'Homoiotherm'. Mammals consumed more food and that's what empowers them to withstand all weather conditions. God wants you to absorb and assimilate more of His words, and meditate on them often and often so you can get a whole lot of his blessings packaged for you. Perhaps, reading and meditating in the words of the Lord gives you access to control your world, it opens your eyes to behold Precious and incredible things that are available for you in his kingdom. You get access to things so cute to your future when you mull over the word of God. Isaac understood the power of meditation when he was of age. He has a concern to have a wife, he lived with the expectation that one day his dream will come to reality. He isolated himself to meditate, while that goes on, his dream came to pass. On a cool evening, Isaac went out to align (meditate or think over) his case with the word of God. While yet he cogitates, the Bible recorded that he beholds: Genesis 24:63-64: And Isaac went out to meditate in the field at the eventide (evening time) and he lifted his eyes and saw, and behold the camel was coming; (64) And Rebecca lifted her eyes, and when she saw Isaac, she lighted off(stopped)the camel. God compelled both to meet when Isaac was pondering his mind over what God says concerning his future. Isaac needed a wife of which he knew nothing about, how will the person look like? which tribe? Beautiful or ugly? Rich or poor home? When will it be? Isaac might have thought all this, but God made it simple as he went out to cogitate. He was at the Campus when the result came. Likewise, the woman(Rebecca)never knew Isaac from Adams. In Genesis 24:65, NIV. The Bible said, and she asked the servant, "who is that man in the field coming to meet us?" "He is my master, "the servant answered. So she took her veil and covered herself. The mind of the Lord is to satisfy our needs and to make sure that problems are solved. Though the father(Abraham) has told the servant where to

get a wife for his son (Isaac) the
Very woman was unknown to Abraham, Isaac, and the servant. But
God knew who she was. And God ordered the steps of the servant,
and Isaac, and Rebecca. Isaiah 26:3-4, the Bible says, thou will
keep him in perfect peace, whose mind is stayed on thee: because
he trusted on thee. Next verse, Trust ye in the Lord forever: for in
the Lord JEHOVA His everlasting strength.

Let's take a look at the book of Psalms 1:2-3, and he said, but his delight is in the law (he calms his mind in God's Word) of the Lord; and in his law, he meditates day and night. Next verse, and he shall be like a tree planted by the rivers of water, that brings forth his fruit in his season; his leaf also shall not wither, and what so ever he doeth shall prosper. The writer used a tree planted at Riverside to illustrate how a believer's life ought to be; because he has his root rooted in the river of water, an endless stream of water. The campus of God's Words the endless progression of His blessings towards His people. 'Those whose mind is connected to the word of God, they shall drive strength, energy, and power from the words which they read. They shall not be affected by the weather conditions of any environment. Homoiotherm, adapt to all weather conditions. homoios which means constant, this means that they have a constant supply of strength from the food substance they consume. Herms which means= heat, means that this set of animals received CONSTANT HEAT. This constant heat supply is the anti-cool - antivirus. Sickness made free, a struggle made free. The word of God supplies a constant and great h e a t that energizes us to live the life of abundance, poverty smashed and having no material possessions crashed. When you dwell your intellect on the word of the Lord, you are made free from the limitations of life. Understand life through the word of God, God has bequeathed a lot of gifts, favor, prosperous things that makes life illuminated in his word. We are the effulgence of God's glory. When you abide by the word, you automatically earn a license to unlimited access to prosperity. See yourself through the word of the Lord, understand who you are through the word. Frame your life with it, align your life with what the word is saying concerning your life. God wants to deliver wealth, wisdom, riches of life into your hands as you press further to read his words. All that you want is in the word of God. What God wants to give you is His word because therein lies glorious things of life. The Bible says, Joshua1:8, This book of the law shall not depart out of thy mouth, but you shall meditate therein day and night, that you may observe to do according to all that is written therein: for then you shall make your way prosperous and then you shall have good success. He said, if you ever wish to have success, then the meditation platform shall be ON in your life. Endotherms (mammals) or warm-blooded animals do not give up to any weather conditions. It doesn't matter the heat or the cool, man is always on the go. Don't give up, press further, become what you want to be through God's Word. When you first read the word of God, it might not make sense to you at first. It may seem boring to you, it might appear to you as if you weren't in God's plan for creation. It might look as if you were born on the backside of life. No! no! no! Hundreds of no! You are in the right place, align yourself with it, your answers are there. Let's take it that you are a woman and you are looking for the fruit of the womb, that's to say a developing fetus in your uterus. And you are believing God for it, then you engage yourself reading the word after some time it seems as if the words are not working for you. In this case, you don't have to give up because your answers are in the corner. On several occasions, we have met with people who say that they have tried to make life easier through faith, love, hard work, fasting, prayers, seed sowing, and many other ways, in the end, therefore, they find it difficult to succeed in life. Then we said to them, 'Is that all? Is that the reason why they should give up!? You don't have to give up because you tried your best to make things work and it didn't work out the way you wanted. Cheer up, my dear friend! See there is a turnaround point for everyone, pray, read, sow, increase your faith, ' if you want to buy a car worth200$, reaching there, the seller said is 250$ and what is left with you is 200$ what will you do? You just have to wait until your money is complete or you add more money so that you can get the car. 'Wait or you add more effort to what you are doing. As long as you are alive and you have a very good vision you will make it, look my dear in the kingdom, things are not done automatically but by process and by continuity'. Let say that you lose your job, or you have financial challenges or you may need money to meet up with one thing or the other. And you are believing God for it, therein, it seems as if nothing is happening, no sign of money, everything looks dishearten, in this light, you don't have to give up. In the Bible when God started creation, the Bible recorded that darkness covered the whole place, was that not a challenge? It was a challenge! But He did not give up on that. You just need to read more (study more) of it, absorb more, download enough, press more ahead, be loaded, get deep into it, let it become part of you, then you shall see God's goodness and mercies coming down upon your life. As necessary as bodybuilding food and energy-giving food is needed in our body to enhance normal body functions. Is recommended that we should take a lot of water regularly and to have a normal proportion of diets; to maintain a normal healthy life style. Likewise, it is expected of us to carry out spiritual activities to maintain a sound Christian life. The Lord God of Heaven and the Earth had charged us to pray all the time, as Hannah did. The Bible has it that Hannah was in bitterness of soul, and she prayed unto the Lord and wept 1 Samuel 1:10. In verse twelve, the BiblerecordsthatHannahcontinuedtopraybeforetheLord.Theword'conti nued'connotesthe word 'nonstop', it means ' press ahead' the Bible helps us to know that Hannah preceded in prayers before the Lord God. Yeah! That's God's desire, that we should continue on the Campus to study his words, day in day out; without a season.

Through that, we can maintain a healthy life m style and keep an active relationship with Him. Now let view it this way, every upcoming child, even an adult, needs bodybuilding food rich in protein, likewise, a pregnant woman or a nursing mother needs an extra amount of both energy giving food and bodybuilding food to help maintain the fetus in the uterus (pregnant women). This helps newly born babies to maintain good health, and adults to retain strength at all times. In this same manner, God's desire is for us to retain stability through His words. The Lord expected us to pertain to spiritual exercises and to feed our spirit with His words so that we might understand His plans for us. He wished that we may increase and wax strong in the spirit as Christ did. The Bible gave us a hint of how Christ gets better in His life as He engaged in spiritual works and activities. In like 2:40 KJV. the Bible said, "and the child grew, and waxed strong in spirit, filled with wisdom: and the grace of God was upon him". On several occasions, we have heard people saying "Jesus Christ started his ministry with prayers and ended up with prayers". That talks about spiritual engagement, activities, and involvement. In all ways, He was involved in spiritual things, for example, Jesus quoted the Bible to the devil in the wilderness, Matthew4:4, "But he answered and said, it is written, man shall not live by bread alone, but by every word that proceeded out of the mouth of God. Yeah! That's a good example that Jesus Christ was a great reader, He has studied the words and absorbed them, and He knew how to make us of it when needed. In Luke 6:12, And it came to pass in those days, that he went out into a mountain to pray, and continued all night in prayer to God. Jesus was involved in several spiritual activities that enabled him to triumph in his ministry. I nMatthew4:2: And when he had fasted forty days and forty nights, he was hungry. By his spiritual engagement, He defeated the devil head to toe, left and right. He became tremendous in the spirit through reading the word of God, prayers, and fasting. That's what God wants from us today and evermore that we may get a whole lot of His Blessing assembled for us. Jesus fully loaded with spiritual nutrients wants us to be loaded as well with the spiritual vitamins and also be fully clothed with the word of God so that we could live and maintain a sound and healthy Christian life.

WHAT TO DO TO ENJOY THE BLESSINGS OF GOD'S WORD IN THE CAMPUS.

1 You must be born again. Born again is a foundation for any believer who wished to make his or her destiny successful in God. Except you be born again; you won't have access to God's blessing, and his goodness. 'Born again is a key, to begin with, God'. in Luke 3:3, Jesus said, … verily, I say unto thee, except a man be born again, he cannot see the kingdom of God. Is wise to know that is not only the kingdom that God has for us as his blessing. There are hundreds and thousands of blessings God has bequeathed to us through his words. When you become born again, you automatically receive the license to partake in God's glory. Being born again is a compulsory subject in the Campus of God's Word. It will help you to gain, gain access, and control over the environmental issues and factors that are fighting your life. Being born again makes you one with the Lord; it units you with the Father; it enables your spirit to mingle with the Holy Ghost. It gives you access to heavenly blessings and also it makes your spiritual person oneness with God. Jesus had prayed about it before He went to the cross; although He referred to those who believe in Him. He said, John 17:21: That they all may be one; as thou, Father, art in me, and I in thee, that they also may be one in us: that the world may believe that thou hast sent me. You must be born again; so that all that God has for you may come to pass. So that you can influence your environment positively and impact Wisdom and knowledge into people's lives. Born again is a primary step to take when you aim to receive from God when you're born

again, you are licensed to command wealth, riches, prosperity, and well-being of life. When you become born again, everything works for you; they respond to you each time you call because you are registered member of the kingdom. 2 Be addicted to the word of God. The word of God is a mirror through which you can see the real you. Let It be part of your life. Stay focused on it. InJoshua1:8, the Bible says, this book of the law shall not depart out of thy mouth, but thou shalt meditate therein day and night, that thou Mayes observe to do according to all that is written therein: for then thou shalt make thy way prosperous, and then thou shalt have success. If you have ever thought about how to illuminate your life; or how to live a prosperous and successful life, then you have to be addicted to the word of God. In Psalms Gospel chapter 1:3, it says, and he shall be like a tree planted by the rivers of water, that brings forth his fruit in his season; his leaves also shall not wither, and whatsoever he doeth shall prosper. As energy-giving food and bodybuilding, food benefits your body; likewise, the words of God nourish your soul. Perhaps, the word of God goes beyond that; it revitalizes your life, your destiny, your business, and every other thing surrounding your environment. It brushes your whole life, your soul, and your spirit. So, you must be addicted to it. Note that the word of God in your spirit helps you to work in the strength of the spirit of God to achieve your goals in life. 3 Develop a personal relationship with God. One of the key ways to get something from God is by keeping a good relationship with him. Your relationship with God will go far better to attract blessings to you than you ever imagine. Most people are enjoying the goodness of the Lord not because of the services they rendered to him but the legitimate confidentiality they have with

him.Love,affection,liberalheart,allthesethingsscorehighinthesightofGo d., In first Corinthians 2:9, the Bible put it this way, "But as it is written, Eye hath not seen, nor ear heard, neither have entered into the heart of man, the things which God hath prepared for them that love him.2:10 But God hath revealed them unto us by his Spirit: for the Spirit searched all things, yea, the deep things of God". Your ability to maintain personal relationships with God opens you up to next-level blessings. It's possible to secure a better future in your affair with God. Jesus maintained a union with the Father, and His work on earth was successful. John 17:21: That they all may be one; as thou, Father, art in me, and I in thee, that they also may be one in us: that the world may believe that thou hast sent me. The Father in the Son and the Son in Us through the Holy Spirit. We are the luminance of God's glory. Your ability to develop personal affairs with your Creator is your chance to gain victory over your environment. Every man has one challenge or the other, your affairs with God determine whether he will help you or not. A good relationship with God is a good thing to keep because that's the Genesis of your well-being here on earth. 4 Earnest prayer: men like Elijah have shown us that we can shape our lives or destinies through earnest prayer. God has given us extra opportunities through prayers to restructure and reframe our lives and works, not just as individuals but also as nations or institutions. Viscosity in a believer's life; more especially praying without a season can usher you into extraordinary blessings. pray earnestly, and build your confidence around your prayers. Giving up too soon may be an indication that you weren't earnest in the first place. When you make your requests known to God, believe that your prayers are granted. Earnest prayers brought Samuel to Hannah, 1 Samuel 1:20, the Bible says, wherefore it came to pass when the time came about after Hannah had conceived, that she bore a son, and called his name Samuel, saying, Because I have asked him of the Lord. Now, consider what the Bible said about her in verse 12: And it came to pass, as she continued praying before the Lord.... She knew that her answer will come if she persists in her request to God. God gives attention to earnest prayers; because He is a prayer-answering God. The Bible says when Ahab went up to eat and drink, and Elijah the prophet went up to the top of the Camel, and he cast himself down upon the earth and put his face in the space of his two-legs. Now the question is what was Elijah doing? I believe that he was speaking in tongues, he was loading bullets in his gun, he was charging his 'power bank' he was fixing things the way they should be, what do you think? 1Kings 18: 41-42.; After three years and six months, Elijah prayed earnestly and the sky poured out water_rain.1 King 18:45. Jesus prayed earnestly, Mark 6:46: And when he had sent them away, he departed into a mountain to pray. When you read the word of God and you follow it up with prayers, you stand thechancetogainalltheBlessingsyoueverneededinlife.I'mprivilegetosay thatifyouarenot prayerful; 90% of what God has for you might not come to pass in your life. Life will make no sense to you until you fix things the way they ought to be. Earnest prayers can usher you into well-being and abundant living. Prosperity, riches, and wealth living are easy to obtain when you attached prayers

. **MAKE A DIFFERENCE THROUGH THE WORD OF GOD IN THE CAMPUS OF GOD'S WORD.**

Every student on the campus is expected to make a positive difference; and influence people positively. Just as children are expected to grow into adulthood, everyone created by God is created to make a disparity. Jesus made a discrepancy so we are not exonerated to make a difference. To understand what we meant, let's take it this way. Naturally, except for identical twins, no human being is exactly alike. Worldwide, human beings vary both in appearance and otherwise. For example, body features such as: Height, =tall, average, or short _the height in meters. Size, =heavy, plump, slim, or stout. Hair, =long hair, short hair, wavy hair, black hair, grey blonde hair. Face look, =round face, long face, smooth face, wrinkled face, or dimpled cheek. Other related body features, tribal marks, or beauty marks. In addition to that, other related body features include the following: Mouth, =thick mouth, red mouth, black lips, or broad mouth. Complexion, =black, ebony black, light complexioned. Eyes=black eyes, dark brown eyes, or blue eyes. Eye brows, =thick eye brow, bushy eye brow, and trimmed eye brow. Nose, =short nose, flat nose, pointed nose, and longnose. These are physical body features in which people differ from each other. Now, let's view the abstract part through which people differ from others. People look unique among others in different ways. We will consider a few of those features and get them explained in details. Character, = someone might take the look of another fellow but portraits different characters. At a look, a son might look like the father, a daughter might look like the mother but they portray different types of lifestyles. Twins might look alike but they have different characters, behaviors, attitudes, or ways of doing things. One may be humble while the other may not. Characters flow from inside; it is the mind that controls the character. The problems facing the world today are primarily caused by the mind-set of people. For peace to reign in this world today, people's minds must be controlled. That's why the Bible says, Proverbs 4:23,"Keep your heart with all diligence; for out of it are the issues(problems)of life. Adequate use of the heart determines the flow of peace around the world. We exist to enjoy the good things of life, but the mixed management of the heart has turned the world into a lethargy. Nonetheless, there is hope for the world, Jesus assured us to give us perfect peace. John 16:33, "These things I have spoken unto you, that in me ye may have peace…". That's where we can have peace in God. 'Naturally, except for the Twins, no human beings are exactly alike. That's why God wants to give us one right-thinking pattern. The world would be a better place If people could learn how to manage their minds(heart). Out of it flows troubles of life and out of it also flows peace of life to those who believe in Christ Jesus (John16:33).

WHAT IS CHARACTER?

Hence, we are attending to the abstract features in which most people differ among others, we will consider the inner definition of character. ' character can be defined as a moral or mental feature that helps to distinguish an individual among others. It is the quality distinctive to an individual. It is the characterization that gives the description or representation and analysis of the main attitude of a person. A character can be developed, a character can be inherent; a character can also be copied. Most family members have different characters, behaviors, attitudes, manners, and unique ways of doing things. That makes some homes differ from others.

TYPES OF CHARACTER

There are various types of characters that people portray that make them different from each other, but we're going to have a few of them explain in this text. A person can be rightly explainedwithwhathe/shedoes_characterhe/shedepicts.Typesofcharacterinclude: **(1)** The static character: this is an inborn attitude, is a type that a person can inherit from his or her parents, it hardly changes, this type of character remains the same from time to time. It takes divine intervention to change. It can be called ' 'born with and died with the character'. In a play or a novel, it can be called ' started with and ends up with character'. In a play or novel, it doesn't change; it remains static. **(2)** A dynamic character: this type of character, is unlike a static character; dynamic character changes. This type of character can be copied from a friend. One can easily change from bad behavior to good behavior. A dynamic character changes. Jesus admonished us to change our characters when he said, "... Repent: for the kingdom of God is at hand"(Matthew 4:17). We must admit dynamic change to suit God's purpose for which we were created. **(3)** Round Character = in life, people practice round character, while some individuals move from good to bad while others move from bad to good. God expected us to change from bad to good and remain stationed in our faith in Him. Round characters are like dynamic characters hence people can display their good and bad traits. **(4)** Minor character= minor character can sometimes have a bigger reward. A minor character is the features that occurred perennial. A minor character is there to assist the major or the main character; the minor character has less influence than the major character. Jesus played major role, he did all that the Father had sent him to do, he obeyed and did as it was written of him. Today He wants us to follow suit. Jesus performed the major role and today he wants us to play the minority part and get bigger rewards. 1 John 2:5: But whoever keeps his word, in him truly the love of God is perfected. By this, we may know that we are in him. Mark 10:45: For even the Son of man came not to be served but to serve and to give his life as a ransom to many. What a great role He had played, today God wants you to make a difference through his words. That's the way to maintain well-being and wealth dividend. Nevertheless, there are several types of characters that are not mentioned here in this text. However, we will in detail illuminate the various ways in which people differ from others. Additionalmeansbywhichpeopledifferamongothersincludethefollowing : Reasoning = no human beings are exactly alike. Every one of us has a different way of thinking, reasoning, behaving, and ways of reacting to issues. Our intellects differ. You may look at an object and give an interpretation relating to what you reason about the object. Another fellow can still look at the same thing and provide different information. Someone might look like the other and have a unique way of thinking or reasoning. For example, when a man married a woman, as they continue to live together, they will start having a facial or resemblance to each other. Despite that, their characters, their reasoning might be different. People from different parts of the world have different ways of doing things, either by belief or by look, traditional, or religious beliefs, and that's the reason why God sent his son to us that he might show us the right way of making a difference through his word. Intonation = people may have the same look, same skin complexion, same body shape, same height, same attitude but might differ in speech pitch or voice. One might speak plainly, boldly enough with smart tones while the fellow might not. For example, the Bible told us that Aaron the son of Amram and Jochebed of the tribe of Levi was three years older than his brother Moses; and God sent Aaron to serve as a spokesman to Moses. Exodus 4: 10: Moses said unto the Lord, O my Lord, I am not eloquent, neither heretofore, nor since thou hast spoken unto thy servant: but I am slow of speech and a slow tongue. Go to verse 16: And he shall be thy spokesman unto the people: and he shall be, even he shall be to thee instead of a mouth, and thou shall be to him instead of God. One way or another, people differ from each other. In the Christian religion, God appointed the fivefold ministry, this shows us that as our faces are different, so also our callings, grace, and works are different. All works and grace Are given for the unity of faith and the work of perfection because God is perfect. Here on Earth, human beings cannot rightly look alike; but God has made us one in his kingdom through Jesus Christ our Lord. Oh! Glory be to God. Amen. However, there are several ways people differ from each other, both men and women. Most of the time, we found out that people from other countries might look alike at sight. For instance, people with fair complexion are mostly identified through their looks (appearance). Some countries differ from other countries through facial expressions, some have tribal marks on their faces, sometimes some persons are identified by the language they speak. For instance, the French-speaking countries, English-speaking countries, and Arabic-speaking countries. Encompassing with other nations or countries which are not mentioned. There are various ways in which people differ from each other. There's also one belief that every black person is of the black countries, and every white person is of the white countries. No! no! no! Not always. Most blacks are from white countries while most whites people are from black countries. Although there are some other means people could be different from their fellow but the above features are concrete and abstract means we can say that humans cannot be the same. However, most individuals inherit the character they live from parent, while others inherit family resemblances such as body shape, skin color, and facial appearance. Most kids take after their parents, grandparents, and other relatives or family members. However, when you humble yourself before God and confess with your mouth and wholeheartedly that God can save you and you believe also that Jesus has risen from the dead as the Bible book of Romans 10:9 puts it. "That if thou shalt confess with thy mouth the Lord Jesus, and shalt believe in thine heart that God has raised Him from the dead, thou shalt be saved". In verse 10 of the same chapter, the Bible said, "For with the heart man believes unto righteousness; and with the mouth, confession is made unto salvation. Now let's consider something unique. When you confess the Lord Jesus Christ with your mouth, and you Concord unto righteousness wholeheartedly; you have called God's attention to yourself. Regarding your dynamic change, God releases his spirit through born again into your life. In this text, we will describe the spirit of your new birth in several ways that will enable us to communicate effectively on how to make a difference through the word of God. It will also help us to Impact deep knowledge of who we are in God and how we can establish a good relationship with Him. When you first come to God, God will give you the spirit of your birth; once you receive the spirit, you are automatically born and registered into the family of God. Once that happens, then you can walk with the consciousness that you are a registered member of God's kingdom. Jesus emphasizes the necessity of the firstborn spirit in the life of every believer that must make his/her way to Heaven. He let us know that those who will be in the kingdom are the registered members only. The spirit of your new birth gives you a new look, a new life, and a new way of doing things. In fact, by it, you gain access to behold the goodness of God's love in your life. A lot more, you also gain the license to enter the kingdom of God, it's stated that on earth no human being is alike to each other. But in God's kingdom, we are one. He is our Father, we are his sons, we are like him, no difference unlike the world pattern of the uniqueness of life. Galatians 4:6: And because ye are sons, God had sent forth the spirit of his Son into your hearts, crying Abba Father. Jesus stated that despite who you are and what you are, except you are born of the spirit you can't enter into the kingdom of God. Most Christians misunderstood this spirit, they always think of it as the spirit that helps you to make heaven or to enter the kingdom or to follow Christ or to do the will of God, and many more, but that's not all about the spirit. However, the spirit of your new birth does all that. Yet the work of the spirit goes beyond that. In this glorious light, we will talk about this spirit in more detail by using words that describe who he Is to us, in us, and for us. Yeah! He does all that. Now, let's refer to Him as ' the spirit of enablement'. The spirit you received after being born of the spirit, as Jesus said, John3:3... verily, I say unto you Except a man be born again, he cannot see the kingdom of God. Next to 6: that which is born of the flesh is flesh, and that which is born of the spirit is spirit. The spirit of your new birth enables you to enter into some dimension of God's blessings. He enables you to see the kingdom of God and to possess it as an inheritance. He enables you to do all things. Philippians 4:13 I can do all things through Christ which strengthened me. He enables you to make a difference through the words of God. It will be a thing of joy to understand what this book is revealing to you. See, when you come to God and you confess your sins, God gives you instant spirit and this spirit that you now have will give you a new way of thinking. The way you think about the kingdom, the way you think about God, and the way you think about yourself, it will make you have Jesus' kind of belief; you don't see things the way others see, it will make you see things the way others could not. Just as we said, for most Christians the work of the spirit ends by teaching them how to make the kingdom of God, or how to know more about God. Yeah! He did all that. But The work of the spirit goes beyond that. You can't have this spirit and become poor in life. Let's move on, do not forget that in this text we called Him the spirit of enablement. He helps you to know when something is wrong in your environment and how to fix it. He gives new understanding; Luke 24:45: then open their understanding, that they might understand the word of the Lord. He enables you to understand what the word of God is saying about yourself and your world. The spirit of your new birth helps you to live a healthy life, He makes you appear special in all things; He put you in front of all good things. He enables you to see what the word of God is for you. Proverbs 4:20, The Bible says, my son, attend to my words; incline thine ears unto my saying. Without the spirit of God, it is impossible to incline your ears unto the word of God, let alone to understand it. As a man, you have hundreds and thousands of things to think about yourself, your family, your work, your relatives, and many more, with all this in your mind, you will find it hard to infer what the word of God is saying. So the spirit of your birth helps you to read, think, and picture what God has for you in his word. Proverbs 4:21: Let them not depart from thine eyes; keep them amid thine heart; (22) For they are life unto those that find them, and health to all their flesh. Is obvious that when you come to God and you humble yourself and submit to his authority, he gives you what I call ' indwelling Spirit. This spirit will dwell in you and make you the temples of the Holy Spirit. 1 Corinthians 3:16 says, "Know ye not that ye are the temples of God, and that the spirit of God dwelled in you ". Glory to God, the place we read stated that you are a mobile temple and also a spirit personified. That means you carry God's presence. This spirit makes his abode in you, His more than identical twins, He goes beyond family resemblance, He doesn't give you the features you inherit from your biological parents, he makes you who you are in God. 'prosperity is as simple as 1,2,3 to achieve when you carry Holy Ghost in your life '. He helps you to see what others could not see; he goes beyond giving you physical qualities or features.

BODY FEATURES DISCRIPTIVE WRDS.

Nose = The short nose, long nose, flat nose and pointed nose.

Face =Round face, long face, broad face smooth face and wrinkled face.

Complexion =, Black color, ebony black color and light complexion.

Size = Slim size, plump size, heavy size, and stout size.

Hair. Long hair, short hair, black hair, and grey hair.

Height. Short, tall, average man or woman.

Eyebrow. Bushy, and trimmed eye brow.

Mouth. Red lips, black lips, thick mouth, and broad mouth.

Eyes. Black eyes, dark brown eyes, blue eyes.

Now hear this, from God's point of view, the spirit goes beyond the physical features listed above. Every member of a particular family has a legal right to claim properties or family belongings. Although in some parts of the world mostly in Africa, things are being shared according to the other members of the family. First son portion of possession, and second son portion of the properties. But in the side of God, once you believe that He is, and He rewards those that diligently seek him, therein, you stand the chance to ask for anything and it shall be done unto you. having understood that, you are entitled to ask, you are entitled to receive, you are entitled to possess God's blessings regardless of your position in your family. In that same regard, the spirit you received after being born again, gives you all God's features such as the Power to dominate your environment, sovereignty to steer up the way things should work in your life. In Genesis 1:28, the Bible says, "And God said unto them, be fruit and multiply, and replenish the earth, and subdue it: and have dominion over the fish of the sea, …". Man lost this sovereignty inthegardenbuttodayGodhasgivenusasecondchancethroughJesus.You rabilitytoreceive Jesus Christ and retain your new birth spirit; takes you back to the sovereignty of God. This enablement spirit is your 'birthright in God'. He enables you to impact changes in people's lives and your environment. He enables you to exploit your business. He enables you to meditate, cogitate, and assimilate the word of the Lord in your spirit. The spirit of your birth gives you a healthy proficiency in what God has for you through His Word. Proverbs 4:22: For they are life unto those that find them, and health to all their flesh. The spirit of God you

Received will enable you to yank life from the word of God to all areas of your life. Most believers don't understand what life is, they think that life is all about a man existing for a longer time on earth. Take note that it is not only the man that needs life; Is wise to understand that you receive life to give life to other things around you. Please note that: your business needs life, your job, your work, and your nation or country, and your environment as well needs life. Even your household. God gave us life that we all might live and transport it to things within us. Think about this: you are alive and your family and your business are dead into trouble, will you have joy or will you be happy? So we are meant to give life to everything as it concerns our lives. Jesus' statement revealed that known living things have voices. So if they have voices, that means that they can grow, and if they can grow, that means you can positively grow things around you. Luke 19:40, "And he answered and said unto them, I tell you that, if these should hold their peace, the stones would immediately cry out". Jesus personified the stones, He let us understand that known living things have life in them; even though we can't see it with our optical eyes; the fact is that as we need life to live, our businesses or jobs or our works need life to grow. So to make a difference in the Campus of your world through the word of God, you must let the spirit of God dwell in you to enable the functionality of your life. Jesus officially declared openly that power has been given unto us to say or ask what we ever wanted. Luke 11:9-10: And I say unto you, Ask, and it shall be given you; seek, and ye shall find; knock, and it shall be open unto you. (10) For everyone that asked received; and he that seeks finds; and to him that knocked it shall be opened. When Jesus hungered for food, he knew that the fig tree was the answer to his need. When he got closer to the tree, he was disappointed, and he ended the existence of the fig tree. Matthew 21:19. When you become a child of God, you automatically receive the spirit of adoption; this spirit adopts you into the family of God where you work with the authority to make a difference through the word of God. He gives you the ability or the authoritative voice of God. By that voice, God called things into being. The spirit of God lives in us whom through Christ we took part in God, that was why the writer of Galatians said, "Galatians 2:20, ... I live, yet not I, but Christ lived in me....".

DISCOVERTHESPIRITINYOU! Colossian 3:10, "And have put on the new man, which is renewed in the knowledge after the image of him that created him". This chapter of the Bible revealed that the spirit of God which was formerly knocked out by sin is now renewed in us through the knowledge of him that made all things. Once you believe in Him and you receive Him into your life; God automatically adopts you through Jesus who is the Knowledge, and the express image of God. John 1:12: But as many as received him, to them gave him the power to become the sons of God, even to those that believe in his name. This chapter of the Bible revealed that there is available power in God Almighty at waiting for those who will say, "Lord Jesus coming into my life". It also revealed that it takes a higher force to receive Jesus Christ because there are other forces disturbing humans not to accept Christ. However, the condition attached to this statement is as simple as receiving Jesus into your life, then other things become secondary. Perhaps, these statements have a greater dividend, once you believe in the Lord and you receive Him into your life, you stand the chance to become the son of God whereby you retain the power to reign in your World. "But like many, as received him, to them He gave power...". You don't have to worry about anything, you don't let anything perturb you; all you have to do is to receive him into your life and that's all. Once you have him, you are licensed to function as a child of God in power and wisdom. Once you do that, you are permitted to make a difference in any area of your life, also you now become light to others. Then you can now transform and modify your environment by the power of the Holy Spirit in you. Regarding that, believing and receiving Christ into your life gives you a greater advantage that differs from the ones you know.

Furthermore, the promise preceded, "... to them gave him the POWER to become the sons of God...". The power you received is enormous and cannot be counted by percentage, or measured by the meter but fully loaded power and authority to make things happen positively in your life and the fullness of His presence. John 1:16: And of his fullness have all we received, and grace for grace. Let's strike a balance between the two verses John 1:16 and John 1:12: As many as received Him, to them He gave the power to become the sons and daughters of God. John 1:16: And of His fullness have we all received, and grace for grace. Do you discover that both verses talk about power (fullness have we all received; as many, as received him), the fullness of power all in your life. So that everyone who want to attain in this life most first receive Him into his or her life. The spirit of which all things were made has been given unto you; with that, nothing shall be impossible to you. The spirit you received through being born again helps you to maximize the power and grace you received when you believed. This spirit constitutes several things that have to do with our inward and outward aspects of life. This spirit plays a vital role in our lives, he enables us to have an enormous knowledge of who we are in Christ Jesus; he lightens our understanding concerning the word of God. All you need to do is to discover if you have him. John 3:6, Jesus said, that which is born of the flesh is flesh and that which is born of the spirit is spirit. He gave us an insight into the inward (the spirit) and the outward (the flesh). He gave us more insight into the spirit which enables us to understand that the spirit modifies us or revamps us to have a good fellowship with the Father. He opens our understanding to know that we are the effulgence of God's glory; he helps us to have authentic fellowship with God. John 4:24, Jesus said, God is a spirit: and they that worship him must worship him in spirit and truth. This is wonderful to worship God with the accuracy of the mind, laying aside all sentiment of the heart. Do you have it? If you have it, then You can't be a failure because you are too loaded with God's sovereignty. Luke 4:18: The spirit of the Lord is upon me because he has anointed me to preach the gospel to the poor, he has sent me to heal the broken-hearted, to preach deliverance to the captives, and recovering of sight to the blind, to set at liberty them that are bruised. The spirit of God helps you to recover your site so that you can see what the word of God is saying concerning your life. Living by the word of God is one of the benefits we can obtain from the spirit of our birth, that's our birthright in God. David said, Psalm 77:12: I will meditate also of all thy work, and talk of thy doings. Is obvious that God expected us to take advantage of the things he has given or the things he has done for us to make exploitation in our lives. David examined the works of God, and by it, he made an impact in his time. You have the power, you have the spirit; so you can heal your business, you can rehabilitate your home, you can put your life in the direction you ever wanted because we are like him. Yeah! As he is so we're. In Genesis 1:26 the Bible said, "And God said, let us make man in our image, after our likeness..."when you are born again, you receive the spirit of adoption through Christ which is formed in you; then you now put on the image of God. After God has adopted you, he will give you the spirit of understanding and your eyes will be lighting to know that you are the effulgence of His glory and that you are wonderfully made and you are a chosen nation. Furthermore, you will know that making a difference through God's Word in the Campus of God's word is possible for you. THERE IS NEED FOR CHANGES BECAUSE GOD HAS CHANGED THE PATTERN OF LIFE FOR US THROUGH HIS SON JESUS. THERE IS POSSIBILITY TO MAKE THINGS HAPPEN IN YOUR CAMPUS (WORLD) EVEN IN YOUR LIFE.WE ARE ONE IN CHRIST.

KEYS TO MAKE WEALTH AT THE RIGHT TIME.

In this part of this book, we are going to critically analyze some essential ways you can make wealth and prosperity at the appointed time because, in every man's life, there is an appointed time. Although there are the fifties and hundred ways in which you can make wealth and prosperity in this modern time. However, we will provide reasonable guidelines for which you

Will understand and practice today. They include the following:

(1) Value Your opportunity: if there are one or two things that take a man to the top, we suggest that the value you place on an opportunity that comes to you is one. To get deep, let's ask, can someone miss his or her opportunity? Yeah! It is possible. Someone sometimes can miss the opportunity he or she has to become what God ordained for him or her. Or what he or she envisioned his/her life to. There won't be anything so exciting or interesting as a divine opportunity, a divine opportunity is a chance created by God to shift your life from level one to the best level as it suits Him concerning your life. But one thing you have to do is to value your opportunity because most opportunities are not static. Opportunities don't appear all the time, they shift, they come to you today hereafter to another individual. Though opportunity can be divinely programmed, that doesn't make it static; if you are not spiritual enough it can move on to another individual. If you are not sensible enough it can still flam out while your eyes are open because God is not a waste; he loves people who value opportunity. Yeah, some people have thought to have one moment of chance in their lives, but it takes a victorious heart to acquire such moments, it takes adventurous intellect to arrest such a period at the right time. Though it might be divinely programmed, it doesn't occur all the time. Most opportunities can be created by an individual or they can come by divine means. However, how you value your opportunity determines if it will be productive to you, or not. Abraham respected the opportunity he had with God and it was counted unto him as righteousness. He knew that that was a great moment to get his need resolved.

Genesis 15:4-5-6. And, behold, the word of the Lord came unto him, saying, this shall not be thine heir; but he that shall come forth out of thine own bowels shall be thine heir; And he brought him forth abroad, and said, look now towards heaven, and tell the stars, if thou be able to number them: and he said unto him, so shall thy seed be; And he believed in the lord, and he counted it to him for righteousness. God gave Abraham an open cheque to make a withdrawal from the children's warehouse of heaven. God said to Abraham come let me show you, behold the sky how many of the stars can your number; as many as possible you can number, that's the number of children you will have. Abraham honored the opportunity and it was commemorated to him as righteousness. Abraham knew that such a moment doesn't come regularly. In the Bible, Elijah had an opportunity to demonstrate the power of God bequeathed in his life. He bolts the sky not to drop nor fall rain by strong prayers.1 Kings 17:1: Now Elijah, who was from Tishbite, in Gilead, told King Ahab, & As surely as the Lord, the God of Israel, lives—the God I serve—there will be no dew or rain during the next few years until I give the word! &. Elijah furiously spoke to Ahab. However, in most cases, opportunities most of the time required physical strength and proficiency to obtain. Most opportunities require faith to make it yours. Most opportunities appear through challenges of life or competition or combat that are before Life. Violence or issues of life can sometimes give room for a great opportunity. Nevertheless, some can at peace come to individuals; perhaps every opportunity that comes to a man is out for something. However, is wise to know that every opportunity that comes your way carries a blessing. It takes divine grace to understand divine opportunities. Elijah the prophet had an opportunity to unfold the power of God in Israel, and to make his name famous in the land. When God manifested his power through fire, the people saw it and they respected God for his great and mighty deed. They undoubtedly believed, acknowledged the God of Elijah and Elijah the prophet. They stoop low and worship the omnipotent God 1King 18 v 39, And when all the people saw it, they fell on their faces: and they said, the Lord, he is the God; the Lord, he is the God. God said to Elijah go now and show thyself to Ahab, 1 Kings 18:1. God told Elijah to go forth that the opportunity has come for Israel to know that He is the only God. Elijah understood what a divine opportunity meant, and he said to Obadiah, "...As the Lord of hosts lived before whom I stand, I will surely shew myself unto him today". Elijah understood that each time the word of God comes to him, a new opportunity or a new level opportunity is equally at the corner. He knew that one instruction from God can take his life to the next level. Elijah knew that if he had neglected to do what God had told him, such an opportunity might not come in 10 years of his life. That was why he insisted that he must do what God asked him to do. He held unto the word of God which he heard, and he acted on it. Though Ahab thought Elijah was the problem in Israel, he was not. 1 king 18:17 Ahab said, "... Art thou he that troubled Israel?". V 18 Elijah answered and said, "I have not troubled Israel, but thou, and thy father's house..."Elijah stood his ground, he knew that God was the way out of Israel. Elijah accomplished his missions, adding to that, he succeeded in his opportunity through God's help. The Bible says the hand of God came upon Elijah; that's to say the spirit of God was upon him, 1 king 18:46, "And the hand of the Lord was on Elijah, and girded up his loins, and ran before Ahab to the entrance of Jezreel". The true God was invisible, but He was functional in the Prophet's life. The spirit of God was mighty upon him because he obeyed God. As a child of God, your life is full of opportunities, you are different, even though they say you are a problem, that shouldn't disturb you, Cheer up! You are God's glory, your case is not yet over; go back and pray as Elijah prayed. 1 King 18: 37-38,"Hear me, Lord, hear me, that these people may know that thou art the Lord God, and that thou hast turned their heart back again; Then the fire of the Lord fell and consumed the burnt sacrifice, and the wood, and the stones, and the dust, and the licked up the water that was in the trench". You are a friend to Christ, therefore, your life is occupied with numerous opportunities. The earliest version is in the Gospel of Mark (10:46–52) which tells us of the cure of a blind beggar named Bartimaeus (literally "Son of Timaeus"). ... As Jesus is leaving Jericho with his followers, Bartimaeus calls out: 'Son of David, have mercy on me!' and persists even though the crowd attempted to silence him. Bartimaeus understood the Importance of opportunity, he never wished to miss such a chance in his life. He knew that if he lost such a chance, he may not have it again. Most of the time, opportunities require physical effort. Jesus went out of Jericho followed by a great number of people after he had healed the blind Bartimaeus, and his disciples joined him. Those men who follow Jesus were not silent at all; they were walking in jubilant and a great noise. Bartimaeus understood that opportunity does not always come, he had to shout so that his voice ought to supersede the voice of the crowd (opportunity obtained by effort). Mark 10:47-48, the Bible says, "And when he heard that it was Jesus of Nazareth, he began to cry out, and say, Jesus, thou son of David, have mercy on me; And many charged him that he should hold his peace: but he cried the more a great deal, thou son of David, have mercy on me". Yeah, that sounds so instructive to most believers who always give up when faced with the issues of life. As a child of God, you don't have to give up on matters of life. The reason is: you can't tell if your next attempt will deliver the next level opportunity into your hands. 49 to 52 of the same chapter says, "And Jesus stood still, and commanded him to be called. And they called the blind man, saying unto him, be of good comfort, rise he called you; And he, casting away his garment, rose, and came to Jesus; And Jesus answered and said unto him, what will thou that I should do unto thee? The blind man said unto him, Lord, that I might receive my sight; And Jesus said unto him, go thy way, thy faith had made thee whole. And immediately he received his sight and followed

Jesus in the way. That revealed that you as a believer, don't have to give up because of the pressure of life or sentimental cases of life. Go after it by faith, value your opportunity so that it will give birth to more opportunities and breakthroughs in your life. Divine opportunities give rise to greater glory in a believer's life. So value every opportunity that comes to you, and you will see the results therein.

(2) Have the eyes of possibility. The real fact about life is how far you can see is how far you can be. If you are in this geographical world, and you don't see the possibility of creating or making things happen in your life; then you are going nowhere. When you program your life with the eyes of possibility; everything becomes possible for you. The reason why most believers stay too long in a situation is that they don't see the possibility of walking out of it or changing it to become a stepping stone or next-level favor. We are highly blessed; God has allowed us to change any situation around us through the course of prayers. Regardless of what the problem is, we can shift it out of the way. Although it might be divinely allowed, the truth is that you can change it. Moses saw the possibility of delivering his people out of Egypt through the word of God. Most opportunities in life require prayers and crying before they can be fully secure. The people of Israel obtained the opportunity to move out of Egypt through hard groaning (crying and complaining). Genesis 2:23-24-25,"... and the children of Israel sighed because of the bondage, and they cried, and their cry came up unto GOD because of the bondage; And God heard their groaning, and God remembered His covenant with Abraham, with Isaac, and with Jacob; And God looked upon the children of Israel, and God had respect unto them. As a child of God, you have to see the possibility of getting out of every bondage around your life. Moses saw the possibility of getting his people out, and he worked towards it. There are a lot of things that might not rightly work for you the way you expect it until you heed to what God is saying about your life through His word. Whenever things seem tough to Moses, he journeys to Mountain to inquire of God; what God has to say concerning their freedom's dream. Moses left his wife Zipporah, and his son Gershom for Egypt to disentangle his people because he saw the possibility in God's word. When the angel visited Mary, he spoke

to her, Mary accepted because she saw the possibility in what God is saying concerning her destiny. She knew that with God, all things are possible. Luke 1:37-38,"For with God nothing shall be impossible; And Mary said, Behold the handmaid of the Lord, be it unto me according to thy word. And the angel departed from her. The words of the Lord are the light to our part. He makes us shine brighter and brighter every day, He helps us to see possibilities in what God is saying concerning us. Moses saw the certainty in what God said concerning his people; Mary viewed what God said to her and she saw the certainty in it, she said,"...Be it unto me according to thy word..."Luke1:38. Except you heed to what the word of God is saying about your life, 90% of what will make you wealthy might not come to you. We were redeemed by his word. We are saved by his word. Perhaps, what you see is what you believe and what you believe is what comes to you. Have the eyes of possibilities towards the word of God in your life. We are blessed in God through Jesus. What do you see? Can you see possibilities all around you? See possibility in every catastrophe of your life, tell yourself with Jesus I can make it. Now see what a certain man said to Jesus and how Jesus spoke possibility to everyone that believed. Mark 9:20-23,"And they brought him unto him: and when he saw him, straightaway the spirit tore him; and he fell on the ground, and wallowed foaming. And Jesus asked his father, how long has it been since this came unto him? And he said, of a child. And oftentimes it had cast him into the fire, and into the waters, to destroy him: but if thou canst do anything, have compassion on us, and help us. Jesus said unto him, if thou canst believe, all things are possible to anyone that believes. Wow! Faithful Lord, you are a wonderful Father! Dear believer, all things are possible for you, to you, and everyone who believeth in Jesus. The father of the young man who was brought to Jesus, brought his son because he saw possibility in Christ Jesus.

The man believed in his heart that it's possible to get his son back to normal if only they can meet with Jesus. Jesus spoke possibility to him because he knew that he was the possibility to all life thought-provoking. The joy of the Lord is our testimony. When we testify to the goodness of the Lord in our lives, God gets excited. God is pleased with us when we live a wealthy life and a prosperous life. It pleased God when we see possibility in Him because nothing is hard for him to do for us. Jeremiah 32:17,"Ah Lord God! Behold, thou had made heaven and the earth by thy great power and stretched out arm, and there is nothing too hard for thee". The power of God can do anything, He made the heavens and the earth within the intervals of 7days, he made all things possible for us in Christ Jesus. All things are possible to God. But you have to see it first with the eyes of possibility because That's where your wealthy life begins.

Sarah the wife of Abraham thought that her case of bearing a child was beyond God's power, she concluded her case to be void, she saw herself too old to partake in God's realm of possibility, she locked up her heart, she closed her eyes of possibility and set her whole heart away from possibility. God has been so merciful, despite the unbelieve of Sarah, GOD came and resumed all that age has locked down in her body that she has to conceive and bear her husband a child. Genesis 18:10-14, "And he said, I will certainly return unto thee according to the time of life; and, lo Sarah thy wife shall have a son. And Sarah heard it in the tent door, which was behind him; Now Abraham and Sarah were old and well stricken in age, and it ceased to be with Sarah after the manner of women; Therefore, Sarah laughed within herself, saying, After I am waxed old shall I have pleasure, my Lord being old also? And the Lord said unto Abraham, wherefore did Sarah laugh, saying, Shall I of a surety bear a child, which am old? Is anything too hard for the Lord? At the time appointed I will return unto thee, according to the time of life, and Sarah shall have a son. There are several opportunities in God that you can behold with your eyes of possibility because there is nothing too hard for God. He loves us so much that he gave us his son that we might live in abundance and fruitfulness. Most believers thought that Jesus came that we may be saved from sin, and that's all. No! Most of us have also said that he came to draw us nearer to the Father alone, it is also said that he came to spread the word of God and to teach the word of God alone. Yeah! All are right. He came and he fulfilled all that was said about Him. But, beyond that, Jesus came to show us the opportunities and the possibilities of life which are gloriously stationed to us in God. We are the effulgence of God's glory, our praise and Worship gives him joy. He gets glorified when we adore His holy name. "We are all that God has", Jesus came to endow us with the power of possibilities with able power, and unending joy, Jesus came so that we can have life because He is the embodiment of life. He said, John 14:6,"... I am the way, the truth, and the life: no man cometh unto the Father but by me" This Life means an eternal life in heaven. Because of Jesus' death and resurrection, we now have a way to be reconciled with God and have eternal life with Him in heaven. But, is that all that God has for us? No! We are highly blessed; Jesus Christ is the greatest gift God has given to us. In him, we have all our problems solved. Jesus came to restore to us the ticket that the thief stole from us

. John10:10, "The thief come not, but for to steal, and to kill, and to destroy: I come that they might have life and that they might have it more abundantly". We see possibility in what Jesus said. Through Him, we gain life abundant. That's beyond imagination, that talks about life here on earth and life after death. That implies both lives here on earth and lives in heaven. Most believers are confused about earthly blessings, some thought that all earthly wealth and riches are canal. But that's wrong to say. It pleases God when we live a comfortable life, a wealthy life, a healthy life, and a glorious life. However, to receive from God, you must have the eyes of possibility (you must see it with your eyes that God can do all things)

And you must serve Him diligently. Deuteronomy 28:1-8,"And it shall come to pass, if thou shalt hearken diligently unto the voice of the Lord thy God, to observe and to do all his commandment which I command thee this day, that the Lord thy God will set thee on high above all nations of the earth. (2) And all these blessings shall come on thee, and overtake thee if thou shall hearken unto the voice of thy God. (3) Blessed shalt thou be in the city, and blessed shalt thou is in the field. (4) Blessed shalt be the fruit of thy body and the fruit of thy ground, and the fruit of thy cattle, the inner of thy kine, and the flocks of thy sheep. (5) Blessed shall be thy basket and they store. (6) Blessed shalt thou be when thou comes in, and blessed shall thou be when thou goes out. There's a possibility in God that you can be rich at any given time; you can become a well-loaded person even here on earth through Christ Jesus because in him are Loaded all the riches and glorious things of life. The last verse of the Scripture where we read informed us that our going out shall be a blessing and our coming in shall also be a blessing. That wasn't the blessing when you make heaven but solely earthly blessings. The blessings of God for us begin here on earth. Perhaps, you are a child of the highest God, the son of King of Kings. However, the ongoing question is, how far can you see? Do you see the possibility in God? Do you believe that all you need is attainable in Him? At the right time of your opportunity, you have to see the possibility that all things are yours. Jesus has uncovered the secret of what we ought to do to access all that we ever need in life.

Mark 9:23, "Jesus said unto him, if thou canst believe, all things are possible to him that believeth". He lets us know what it takes to make things possible in our lives. He revealed that by believing we make all things possible. What you see is what you believe and what you believe is what you possess and that becomes the possibility of your life. Your ability to believe that God can do it, is rightly your chance to get what you ever needed in life. So behold it first. (3) Have a solemn concordance with God's Word. The power of God's Word might not be functional in you until you agree to what God is saying concerning your life. Many Christians have denied themselves the benefit attached to God's Word because they stare at it but they hardly agree with it. Whichever means the word of God comes to you either by reading or by hearing; the fact that you receive it with a clean heart, it will work for you, the word of the Lord comes to upload new updates of blessing, increase and elevate your life. The writer of Ezekiel revealed that the word of God is received into our hearts and is being heard with our ears. Ezekiel 3:10, "Moreover he said unto me, son of man, all my words that I shall speak unto thee receive in thy heart, and hear with thy ear". When you hear the word of God with your ears and you receive it into your heart with joy, and you allow it to make abode in your life, then it will begin to stimulate your spirit to see several opportunities and possibilities of making your ways prosperous and your eyes will be open to behold new things at waited for you even before you were born. The writer of Hebrew tells us some qualities of God's Word. He said that the word of God is: "quick and powerful, sharper than a two-edged sword". Also, nothing can escape from it once you proclaimed it. The blessings that God has for us are being stored in his word. That's why when you read it with a calm mind, you grow up in knowledge. The blessings of God to us are not coincidence blessings but a potential blessings arranged to elevate our lives to the next level of favor. The writer of Joshua had revealed unto us a crucial secret of what we ought to do to make success and to live a wealthy life. Firstly, he let us know that by consistent meditations we shall discover some instructive guides to abide by as it turns out to better our lives. Secondly, he let us know that by so doing, we shall illuminate our ways and make it prosperous; he let us to know that we can retain a healthy life and success to ourselves. Joshua 1:8, "This book of the law shall not depart out of thy mouth; but thou shalt meditate therein day and night, that thou Mayes observe to do according to all that is written therein: for then thou shall make thy ways prosperous, and then thou shall have a good success". In the first part of the verse we read, the writer advised that we should read it and say it all the time. Also, you have to Speak it to yourself; to your business, and your household at all times. The words have life in them, they are spirits full of power. The following statement advises that we should ponder our minds day after day. When you think over the word of God and you Concord with what it said about your life, automatically, it will begin to work progressively in your life. It helps us to have a deeper insight that we are not just mere mortals but peculiar people. An important key to this is meditation. Just as the Holy Spirit throbbed upon the earth during the creation of things. When there is a situation you want to change, take out time to meditate on God's Word. Within that period of meditation, there will arise in your mind an inspired word to motivate God to move in your life. Many Christians read the word but they don't agree on the word. That's why it doesn't work out the way they wanted it to be. Hosea 14:2 says, "Take words with you… "what do you want in your life? Do you want the opportunity or possibility of life? Is it an appointed time, or do you want to make it at the right time? The key to getting all that you ever needed in life is: don't focus your mind on your current situation rather give more attention to the word of God. Where we read says' ' take words with you". The Bible says without Him was not anything made that was made! So, it is not what is before you that matters but what you say that counts. God was in the midst of the darkness when he commanded the light to shine. Wow! Glory to Jesus! We are like him that made all things, yeah, you are created in His image and His likeness, with His knowledge in your spirit, and His Word in your mouth; you can create opportunities and possibilities real in your life. You can obtain wealth at all times through your belief in God. There's a possibility that with the help of God you can get to your place in destiny. Although the proper use of the word in it standard brings active function of it. This Is because the words that are spoken unto us are spirit . And your agreement with the spirit determines how far it will work for you. In John Gospel 6:63-64, Jesus said, "... The words that I speak unto you, they are spirit, and they are life". This's to say that as you hear the word with your ears, and you receive it with your heart; then the spirit therein deliberately forms a thought that will impact understanding to you. If you are addicted to the word of God, you will observe that each time you read it, you will have joy overflow. This Is because the spirit embedded into the words in which you read is life and they transfer into your heart joy evermore. That's why (Hosea 14:2 says, Take with you word…). Most Christians don't take the word with them. As a believer, your part is to go with the word, ' that's how it works, you speak the spirit into action. Let's critically examine what the writer of 2nd Corinthians 4:13 says," We have the same spirit of faith, according to as it is written, I believed, and therefore have I spoken; we also believe, and therefore speak. The truth is that everything in this life, physical or spiritual can hear and obey God's Word, regardless of the situation. That means if you are facing one challenge or the other, and you are not speaking the word in faith to the situation; you are simply saying that you are comfortable with it. You don't receive the word of God to be quiet. If you don't speak it or respond to it, the word will do you no good. Having a solemn agreement with the word, or responding to the word means more than saying what God has said. You have to see the opportunity therein with your eyes of possibility; then you Concorde with the word and speak something consistent with what He had said. However, the keys are: you have to see the possibility in what God is saying in his word before it can actively work for you. You have the keys to make use of it. Your key to making wealth in this current time is entirely fixed in your understanding of God's Word. Jesus said the words he speaks to us are spirit, which means the more you study it the more you get a whole load of it. God and His Word are one, He talks through his word most of the time. Everything God wishes to tell us is being done through his word. His speaking may come as direction or instruction or a way out of problems. Pondering your mind on God's words, and having an agreement with His Word, can help you excel in Destiny. So make it more substantial and stable in your life. That alone results in the quick delivery of your Blessed package at the right time of your destiny. Glory to Jesus whom God has given unto us as our inheritance. Jesus the word of God is our inheritance. Most Christians don't take much advantage of God's creative power embedded in His words to reframe their lives and environment. Jesus said, the words that I speak unto you, they are spirit, and they are life (John6:63). So, being born again enables us to partner with God. Jesus wants us to understand that the word we read or hear is not an ordinary word but spirit outpouring and life transporters. God spoke things that we see today into being as if they were made by what does appear. Hebrews 11:3, the Bible says, through faith, we understand that the worlds were framed by the word of God so that things which are seen were not made of things that do appear. God constructed the world by the words He spoke. In the verse where we read, we realize that God possibly made His work of creating success through the word of His mouth. When God wanted to further the work of creation, He said what He wanted to see and it came to pass that all appeared unto Him as He wanted. Genesis 1:3, the Bible says, And God said, let there be light: and there was light. Now, in verses 4 of that same Genesis the Bible says, And God saw the light, that it was good…. Now, we find out what happened in verse 3, God said what he wanted, and in verse 4, He saw the evidence of what he has said. The Bible further says, And God saw that the light was nice. Now, when we read back the book of Hebrews 11:3, we discovered that the things which are seen were not made of things which do appear. That means that every word of God we read or hear from audio tapes has the potential possibility to provoke that which we desired to come into being as though they were. So, when we have a solemn agreement with the word we received from God, we are licensed to speak things that we have wanted to reality because the words are spirit. So, see it as an opportunity to get what you want from the realm through the power of God's Word. (4) Get wisdom or ask God for it. One key fact about wealth and prosperity is to get it and to retain it. NOTE:

'YOU CAN'T GET WEALTH OR RICHES AND RETAIN THEM PROPERLY IF THE WISDOM IS NOT FIRST GIVEN TO YOU'.

As we human's need's care, our riches or wealth need's maintenance also. If you don't give much attention to your source of income sooner or later it will downgrade to a low level. 'God can't give you wealth if the wisdom to grow it has not been given to you'. This Is because God is not a waste. Matthew14:20," They all ate and were satisfied, and the disciples picked up twelve basketfuls of broken pieces that were left over". Note that most people who have wealth, might not necessarily know how to maintain it. The disciples of Jesus knew that it is not what you spend that actual account but what you gather up and what you have is what account. Appropriate financial management is what keeps an organization growing; mismanagement can bring down an organization. An excellent way to maintain a wealthy life is your ability to preserve leftovers, the ability to assemble the remnants determines how the future would be. Jesus knew the needfulness of the remnant He allowed His disciples to assemble the left over bread and fishes. Mark6:43: And they took up twelve baskets full of the fragments and the fishes. No restriction on wealth-making and prosperity making in God, how far you go in life is mainly on you; wealth and prosperity are some of the things God uses to decorate life. Wealth and prosperity give life meaning. And God blessed Abraham in all things (Genesis 24:1). However, to accomplish your dreams in life, you need the wisdom of God to dwell in you. Exodus 31:1-3, the Bible says, And the Lord spoke unto Moses, saying, See I have called him

By name Bezalel the son of Uri, the son of Hur, of the tribes of Judah: And I have filled him with the spirit of God, in wisdom, and understanding and knowledge, and all manner of workmanship. (5) And in the cutting of stones, to set them, and in carving of timber, to work in all manner of work man ship. Wisdom and knowledge are in need in our today's world. In all aspects of life, wisdom and knowledge are important to maintain continuity of life. It's compulsory to ask for wisdom because the Bible had told us that: "Wisdom is the principal thing; therefore, get wisdom: and in all thy getting understand"(Proverbs 4:7). God had given Bezalel His Spirit which has the wisdom and knowledge and understanding in all aspects of his work. God gave Bezalel wisdom to make him wealthy and prosperous in his career. There's no doubt that Bezalel could cease to function appropriately in his field of work if not by the best leads of God's spirit in wisdom or proficiency, and understanding. God gave him His spirit to enable him to maintain superiority in his work man-ship. Responsibility or job, career, or business can sometimes be baffling if wisdom and knowledge are not at work. The success of Bezalel wasn't tied to the cutting of the stone nor the carving of the timbers but in God's spirit which supplies unlimited wisdom that enables him to run his work simultaneously. When such a thing happens, we then know That an excellent spirit is doing excellent things in the life of a man and that's what God has chosen to give us through his word. The words of God are the unfolded spirit of God in wisdom, which today has been revealed unto us through His Son. God sent his word to us that we may have all that we needed in life through Him because all things were made by Him.

John 1:1-3: In the beginning was the Word and the Word was with God, and the Word was God; the same was at the beginning with God; All things were made by him and without him was not anything made that was made. All you ever need in your life is the word, because, by His word existence came into being. Wisdom to accumulate wealth and prosperity are all packed in God's Word. It should be obvious that when wisdom is out of place, things go awkward. To stay away from wisdom is to stay out of wealthy living. All things were made by Him. The Bible book of Proverbs 3:19-23 says, "The Lord by wisdom had founded the earth; by understanding had He established the heavens. The book of Proverbs where we read has shown us that the work of creation wasn't a work done by inaccuracy but a calculated work of wisdom. God operated by wisdom and that talks about the creativeness of God in wisdom. It is possible to establish wealth through wisdom and understanding as God had founded the earth and established heaven by understanding. Today, several believers don't understand the benefit of divine knowledge because the spirit of God in wisdom has not been filled in them. God told Moses that He has filled Bezalel with His spirit in wisdom and all manner of work man-ship. Wisdom and knowledge makes it easy to obtain a quick result in whatever thing you are doing in life. God has to operate in wisdom before He could see things happening the way He had wanted. Likewise, if you wished to have a good result in most areas of your life, apply wisdom. God's word is filled with wisdom, knowledge, and understanding. Every word that proceeds from the mouth of the Lord is clothed with wisdom. The truth is that: you have the wisdom of God in you because it is always there for you, but one thing is certain: accurate use of wisdom determines how productive it will be for you. So you need to understand the proper use of wisdom in your life because the spirit of the Lord is upon you, so You just need to believe it and accept it, then you watch out for what the result is going to be. The Lord God of heaven and the earth has possibly made all things by wisdom. Proverbs 3:19-23: The Lord by wisdom had founded the earth; by understanding had he established the heavens. That's the will of God for you that you should also function in the same manner as Him. This is because we are Like him, He has made us with His image.

Genesis 1:27 says, "So God created man in His image, in the image of God created him; male and female. So we are perfectly made, there's no imperfection in us, all that we ever need to make life exciting has been given to us. The Bible made us to know that after God had finished His work; He crossed checked it and found out that all that He had made was good. Genesis1:31 says, "And God saw everything that He had made, and behold, it was very good...". So God is expecting you to operate with His spirit which you have received. The spirit of God passes all understanding to any man who believes in Him. The Bible says, And the child grew, and waxed strong in spirit, filled with wisdom: and the grace of God was upon Him. The child waxed strong in spirit and was filled with wisdom, that reminds us what God did unto Bezalel which he said, And I have filled him with the spirit of God, in wisdom, and understanding and knowledge, and all manner of workmanship. The child was filled with wisdom; Bezalel was filled with wisdom as he received the same spirit of God in which the child thrived in fullness. God wants us to be filled with wisdom because wisdom is the principal thing. God's Spirit filled us with wisdom, knowledge, and understanding so that we can through it maximize all the good things of life that surround our environment. We are highly favored with things God has made for us. We are entitled to speak things into reality as it concerns our life. So speak the word into action because all things were made through it. John 1:1 says, In the beginning, was the word, and the word was with God, and the Word was God. The understanding you receive from the word of God and how you engage with it helps you to live a life of exploits. The world began by the word and by it all knowledge, and wisdom was made. The word was with God and the Word was God and all things were made by Him. Divine wisdom, knowledge, and efficiency to create and to make, to build, and to maintain things in all phases of life both Pure, gentle, and fruitful wisdom to live a peaceable life are the product of the spoken word of God's mouth. James 3:17 says, But the wisdom that is from above is first pure, then peaceable, gentle, and easy to been treated, full of mercy and good fruits, without partiality, and hypocrisy. That's wonderful to receive, pure, peace, mercy, and good fruits. However, the accurate function of the word in your life is in your hands, because how you engage with the word of God will fully determine how it'll work for you. The fruit of God's wisdom is restricted only to those who have the spirit of God. Bezalel was filled with the spirit of God in wisdom, knowledge, and understanding, Exodus 31:3; likewise, the account of Jesus the Bible records that the child grew and waxed strong in spirit and was filled with wisdom. God by wisdom founded the earth; and by understanding had He established the heavens, Proverbs 3:19. It's essential to know that you can receive wisdom from God when you ask because Jesus said, "... ask and it shall be given you...". So your relationship with the Son matters most. In this light, to make wealth, and to maintain it you need to assemble wisdom first. we ought to glance deeply into the word of God to discover the keys and chief principles that Jesus employed for the effective use of wisdom. God committed to his work during the making of things. He showed concern to finish His project before he could have rest. The Bible says, Genesis 1:31, And God saw everything that he had made, and, behold, it was very good. And the evening and the morning were the six days. God took the responsibility for His heart's desire to come to reality. It was God's heartbeat to bring creation into finished. Genesis 2:2 the Bible says, and on the seventh day God ended his work which he had made, and He rested on the seventh day from all His work which He had made. The Bible records that God founded the earth by wisdom, and by understanding he established the heavens. God did not give us dumping wisdom that we should dump but He gave us dominant wisdom that we might establish and make an exploit here on earth. We have to be committed to providing good results in all areas of our lives. The underlined words show that God breaks from his work after he might have finished His work. He was committed to the project and He wished not to rest until he arrived at a positive point, and that's what God is expecting from us today. He wished that we should move ahead and never get worried. He wants us to be rooted and be strong in the spirit and be filled with wisdom. The Bible book of Luke 2:40 the book recorded that:"...The child grew, and waxed strong in the spirit, filled with wisdom...". He grew up, He became more responsible for the works that God has committed into His hand, and He became committed to His father's work. John 4:34 says, Jesus said unto them, my meat is to do the will of him that sent me and to finish his work. Wisdom makes you responsible; Jesus committed to finishing the work of His Father, it was after God had finished his work, he rested. Likewise, Jesus, after He finished His work, He gave up to the ghost. John 19:30 The Bible says When Jesus, therefore, had received the vinegar, he said, it was finished: and he bowed his head, and gave up the ghost. Divine wisdom makes you responsible for your destiny and it makes you more committed to doing the will of God. Through love and kindness, God filled Bazele with excessive wisdom and understanding. Exodus 31:3-5, And I have filled him with the spirit of God, in wisdom, and understanding, and knowledge, and all manner of workmanship; To devise cunning works, to work in gold, and silver, and brass; And in the cutting of stones, to set them, and in carving of timber, to work in the manner of work man ship. The underlined word shows an excellent man operating in an excellent spirit doing excellent things. Those who purely believed in Christ Jesus shall receive it. In as much as you believed, the spirit of wisdom will make His abode in you and help you to live a glorious life. Divine wisdom enables you to do great and mighty things. Before that, you ought to change your mentality, start thinking like a King's child. Because the way you thinking mostly determines how the spirit works with you. God has not Limited us to anything but we can sometimes limit ourselves. We are rated high before God; we are bought with a price; God has not hated any man. He loves us in a way that He has to give us His Only Son to die for us. We carry His image. He loved us more than any other creature that He had made. That's the reason why He gave us dominion over all things. Genesis 1:28. But the truth is if you don't realize that you are a king's child, you might stay away from his blessing as it concerns your life. Also, you might be missing out on his purpose for your life. That was the reason why He gave us the wisdom to help us realize who we are in Him. He gave us the wisdom to make us accountable for all things. Though the plan of God in creation wasn't for us to be poor. He has blessed us with all heavenly and earthly blessings. James 3:12 the Bible says, who is a wise man and endured with knowledge among you? Let Him shew out of a good conversation his works with meekness of wisdom. In Ecology, the climate of a locality changes during the year, and these changes affect the plants and animals living therein. Though changes occur in the plant and animal population of a territory, yet you as a child of God are not lost to changes in your ecosystems, regardless of the circumstances in your nation or country, you are set apart by wisdom. Perhaps wisdom helps you to distinguish when things go wrong in your life, yet things might go the wrong direction, nonetheless, you are not Lost in the crowd. Possibly, effective use of wisdom distinguishes you among the multitude. Though you might be humble, submissive, meek, and patient yet you are not gull over environmental issues. However, knowledge, wisdom, and understanding help's you to coordinate things in a conceptual framework or scheme of work. The truth remains that divine knowledge and understanding make you reproductive in all your endeavors. Good wisdom enables you to carry out your work with meekness, humbleness, and full of good fruits and peace of mind. James 3:17: But the wisdom that is from above is first pure, then peaceable, gentle, and easy to be entreated, full of mercy and good fruit, without partiality, and without hypocrisy. Wisdom is given by God; wisdom is a spirit when we read the word or hear the word of God through audio tapes or books, and we believe what we read, then we shall have whatever we asked for because the spirit will be transferred into you by what you hear. We have nothing of ours if not given to us by God through Jesus Christ. We received the spirit of wisdom by receiving Jesus into our lives, God the Father of all has given us all things as it pertains to life. Ephesians 1:17: That the God of our Lord Jesus Christ, the Father of glory, may give unto you the spirit of wisdom and revelation in the knowledge of Him. All things were made by him, Perhaps He is the word in the making of things we see and things not seen. There are tremendous blessings we can obtain from God through His Son. GOD began life for mankind many years ago, even when the earth was in a vacuum state when the planets was devoid of matters, yet He created space for the existence of man. God gave man dominion over the universe including other planets. God had given us the spirit of wisdom, and revelation in the knowledge of His son that we may adopt the mind of possibility in our environment. Although, sometimes we can be affected by some environmental topics, nonetheless, he has given us the capacity to analyze any topic of life provided we operate in divine wisdom and knowledge. Is obvious that sometimes we can be affected by some changes in our spiritual environment, and occasionally we can also be influenced by some changes in our external environment. For instance, when Ahab narrated the story of what Elijah the prophet had done to other prophets with his sword to Jezebel, then Jezebel's response to what he heard from Ahab, made Elijah run. Life became intolerable to Elijah the prophet when he saw some changes in his external environment; he echoed out to God to have his life taken. 1 king 19:1-4: And Ahab told Jezebel all that Elijah had done, and withal how he had slain all the prophets with the sword; Then Jezebel sent a messenger unto Elijah, saying, So let the gods do to me, and more also if I make not thy life as the life of one of them by tomorrow about this time; And when he saw that, (Elijah reacted) he arose, and ran for his life, and came to Beer-Sheba, which belonged to Judah, and left his servant there (self-defense); But he went a journey into the wilderness, and came and sat down under a juniper tree: and requested for himself that he might die; and said, it is enough; now, I oh Lord, take away my life; for I am not better than my fathers. Elijah's reaction to what Jezebel had said was the fact that we can sometimes be influenced by some factors in our external environment. Changes in the outside part of our lives can deeply express how we felt on the outward. Elijah said "it is enough ", which means he couldn't accommodate depression any longer he had to tell God to take away his life. But today our case is quite different, we have a lot of devices, our systems are filled with blessings. We are operating in a triumphant system. We have been given the spirit of wisdom, we have the comforter with us, we can regulate any matter that wants to refute our peace. Elijah never knew how to swivel his condition into wealth-making. Why he asked God to take a way his life, God was busy preparing something to get his life restored unto him. 1 King 19: 5-6: And as he lay and slept under a juniper tree, behold, then an angel touched him, and said unto him, Arise and eat; And he looked, and behold, there was a case based on the coals, and accuse of water at his head. And he did eat and drink and laid him down again. But for ourselves today, it is not so. You don't have to lay down when depression and frustration are upon you because you have the Holy Ghost with you all the time, He fills you with powers all the time, His presence in your life is powerful (Acts 1:8). He releases the wisdom of God upon your life all the time. Jesus called him a comforter: And I will ask the Father, and he will give you another Counselor to be with you forever-- (John 14:16). He is our counsellor, you have to understand that you are not alone, He is within your environment always: ...But you know him, for He lives with you and will be in you (John 14:17). Note that Jesus alone in your life is a comforter and the Holy Spirit is another comforter. So you have all it takes to end every battle of your life. You are too loaded with blessings; you don't have to be afraid. So, with that consciousness in your mind, you are a hero, even though things got awkward around your system or it appeared that the network of your life has been hacked by the devil, then you don't have to worry about that because the wisdom to gain victory in such a mess is upon you now and forever more. Jesus assured us of victory, He said I have overcome the world: "I have told you these things, so that in me you may have peace. In this world, you will have trouble. But take heart! I have overcome the world" (John16:33). We are highly blessed in God, He has given us the wisdom to change things in our nation, we are meant to live a life of abundance in this world, He gave us a mouth to speak things into reality. He has given us the mouth and the wisdom which our opponents cannot withstand. You have all it takes to make things right in your life. Jesus said in the Bible book of Luke21:14-15, "Settle it therefore in your hearts, not to meditate before what you shall answer; For I will give you a mouth and wisdom, which all your adversaries shall not be able to gain say nor resist. Most believers spend much of their time thinking about themselves, what to eat and what to drink; but Jesus let us understand that is not every time that we ought to think. When Elijah faced depression under a Juniper tree thinking about himself, God sat in heaven and arranged a survival meal for him. God knew that it wasn't a time of taking a thought (1 King 19:4-5-6). Your case might be quite different from that of Elijah, it might not necessarily be a tribunal case or judiciary case, or a case of denying Christ or bread and milk, it might be a case relative to your life or your environment_ an emotional case. For example, Health challenges, or financial challenges, or some other factors that influence your life. Note: 'It is better to be healthy, and stay without food than to be in abundance of food but bad health conditions'. Note also that a man can stay without a phone in his hand but cannot stay without money in his pocket'. Secondly, Jesus said, He will empower your mouth and He will put upon your wisdom to get rid of unwanted gadgets around your life. Thirdly, He said, your adversaries shall give no affidavits nor make utterance or resist your speaking. Jesus has assured us that when we are met with issues of life within our ecosystems or our environment, be it health issues or financial issues, or any issues associated with human life, he would empower our mouth, and put in us the wisdom which when we shall say to our opponents or problem before us out and it will obey us. That's to say that you can change any uncomfortable situation around you through the speaking word of your mouth and effective use of wisdom. That's to say, you can say to scarcity stop or you can say to your body be healed now or you can say to your adversary depart out of my way and it shall be done. ' Every man born on earth has an environment, and can sometimes be influenced by environmental factors. Now, When Jesus was in his environment doing the work of His Father, environmental factors agitated against him, and He was brought to Pilate by the soldiers and before Pilate was a great multitude of men and women, children and old men who were yelling to crucify him. Then Pilate before the congregation now asked Him saying: "Art thou the king of the Jews? "Then Jesus answered and said, "thou says it". Pilate could not gain a saying unto His answer, then Pilate turned to the congregation and said: "I find no fault in Him". Like 23:1-4: And the whole multitude of them arose, and led him unto Pilate; And they began to accuse him, saying, we found this fellow perverting the nation, and forbidding to give tribute to Caesar, saying that he is Christ a King; And Pilate asked him, saying, Art thou the king of the Jews? And he answered him and said, thou says it; Then said Pilate to the chief priests and the people, I find no fault in Him. There are hundreds of things that can accuse your belief even in your environment. Most of the

time challenges of life can come to ask you a question such as: are you a child of God? Are you a believer? You ought to know that the multitude led him up to Pilate and they accused him of several things. Regardless of what was accused of him, Pilate could not have access to his answer. The good news is that Jesus has given us a mouth and all the wisdom required to eliminate all the mountains and red seas that accuse our belief in God. Luke 21:15: For I will give you a mouth and wisdom, which all your adversaries shall not be able to gain say nor resist. Jesus is saying that he has done it before, and he will do it again and again for you. He did it unto Pilate and Pilate could not say anything against him. He is letting us know that we can speak and nothing will resist us. It wasn't a promise but a fact. He knew that one born of a woman in this world is faced with troubles, but look at what He said to us, Luke 16:33: These things I have spoken unto you, that in me ye might have peace. In the world ye shall have tribulation: but be of good cheer, I have overcome the world. That's to say, in him we have peace. He Instructed us to be of good reasoning because he has overcome our environment. Does that statement sound like a statement spoken by someone who doesn't know the situation of life? No! He let us know that tribulations are always available within our world. Then He further let us know that peace can only be attained in him. He communicated to us what he had done for us. He let us understand that regardless of any challenges a round u; he has overcome them all. It makes no difference what the matter is; all you need to do is to be conscious that you can neither fell nor lose; that's why He gave us His presence. John 14:18: I will not leave you comfortless: I will come to you. In Matthew 28:20, Jesus said, "I am with you always, even unto the end of the world. Amen.

Glory to God! We are comforted by the presence of the Holy Ghost. What incomparable confidence we have in him because He has given us His everlasting presences that's the reason He told us that whatever we ask in His Name He will do it. John 14:13-14: And whatsoever ye shall ask in my name, that will I do, that the Father may be glorified in the son; If ye shall ask anything in my name, I WILL DO IT. The statement above is not a promise, it's a fact. We are highly blessed with His presence and his wisdom. There is a possibility that when you ask anything in his name, He will course it to happen as you wanted. God is never weak nor tried to give ear to our complaints, He is ready to help us at all times.

ACKNOWLEDGE GOD IN EVERYTHING. What is an acknowledgement and how can it benefit you? Acknowledgement Is the act of recognizing someone or something, it means giving honor, respect, recognition, and praise to someone whom you think that deserves it. For example, God being our creator and our provider, He deserved to be acknowledged. Perhaps, how you acknowledge an authority determines whether it will work for you or not. How you recognize or how you acknowledge your boss, your husband, your wife or authority is what will determine if it will benefit you or not. Our God is good, he deserved respect, honor, thanks, praise, and acknowledgement. This is because, how you understand the help of God in your life is what will make God bless you. So acknowledgement will benefit you If you learn how to honor God in your life. Trust in God with all your heart, acknowledge him all the time so that He will pour down His blessings upon you. Proverbs 3:5-6; the writer of Proverbs advises us saying, Trust in the Lord with all your heart; and lean not unto thine own understanding; In all thy ways acknowledge him, and he shall direct your part. God is too faithful to cease to function, several believers redirected their focus away from God because they could not understand the power behind acknowledgement. Notwithstanding, it is your honor and your dependence on Him that foretell how extent your exploitation would be. The blessing of God is ours forever, but we must first dedicate our whole heart to him as our creator. To acknowledge God in all your ways, mainly in your businesses is to say 'yes' to your next level of lifting. God's divine direction is what you need to excel in destiny. Through God's divine direction, Isaac the son of Abraham found Rebecca his destiny wife. Genesis 24:63-67: and he lifted his eyes, and saw, and, behold, the camels were coming; And Rebecca lifted her eyes, and when she saw Isaac, she lighted off the camel; For she had said unto the servant, what man is this that walked in the field to meet us? And the servant had said, it is my master: therefore, she took a veil and covered herself, And the servant told Isaac all things that he had done, And Isaac brought her into his mother Sarah's tent and took Rebecca, and she became his wife, and he loved her: and Isaac was comforted after his mother's death. A rich source to get to your helper's location is to: acknowledge God in all your ways, trust in him with all your heart, and put all your endeavor in him. The divine direction had made marriage simple unto Isaac because his father had initially committed his marriage journey into God's hand. Genesis 24:7: The Lord God of Heaven, which took me from my father's house, and from the land of my kindred, and which spoke unto me, and that swore unto me, saying, unto thy seed will I give this land; he shall send his angel before thee, and thou shalt take a wife unto my son from thence. The writer of proverbs understood the divine direction that was the reason why he said, "... In all thy ways acknowledge Him, and He shall direct your part" (Proverbs3:6). Abraham knew that his servant wouldn't have gotten what he had desired to his son if not by divine lead. That was the reason why he said, "...God shall send His angel before thee, and thou ...". We won't afford all that life needs if God is not involved, it is God who affirms all that we ever need in life. God is our assistance in all areas of our lives, we have nothing to disturb about; he is sufficient to us. 2 Corinthians 3:4-5, the Bible says, "And such trust have we through Christ to God-ward: Not that we are sufficient of ourselves to think anything as of ourselves; but our sufficiency is of God. God is our sufficient, He made all things and by his love and kindness, he has single-handedly given all that life demands of us. It's grateful for us to celebrate and to appreciate God's endless blessings in our being, hence we were created to enjoy life. We ought to agree with God and accept His son into our lives to retain unlimited blessings. The whole duty of a believer is to believe in Christ Jesus whom God has given unto us for us to honor because by him we obtain heavenly blessings and through him, we are rewarded with blessings above and beneath the surface of the earth. John 7:38, Jesus said, "He that believeth on me, as the scripture had said, out of his belly shall flow rivers of living water.

There are two significant statements we needed to understand in this verse. He said, "He that believeth on me as the Scripture had said". He was talking to those who read and agreed with what the Bible held about him. He affirmed to us that whatever the Scripture says about him is true and that He will act on what the Scripture says about him to make it come to pass. That was the reason why He said in John 14:14,"If you shall ask anything in my name, I will do it". This means that if you demand anything in his name, he will compel it to happen the way you wanted it. That wasn't a promise but an assurance of real fact. If you have read anything about him in the Scripture you should hold unto it; because therein is life. Before we move to the second part of the statement, you ought to know that Whoever reads the Scripture and believes

what the Bible says about him, in them, will he put the spirit of God.
But let's read what the Scripture says about him, Hebrew 1:1-4:
God, who at sundry times and in divers manners spoke in time past
unto the fathers by the prophets; Hath in these last days spoken
unto us by his Son, whom he hath appointed heir of all things, by
whom also he made the world; Who being the brightness of his
glory, and the express image of his person, and upholding all things
by the word of His power, when he had by himself purged our sins,
sat down on the right hand of the Majesty high; Being made so
much better than the angels, as he had by in heritance obtained a
more excellent name than they. The second part of the Scripture
(John 7:38) says, out of his belly shall flow rivers of living water.
Jesus referred to the Blessed Spirit of God which those who read the
Scripture and believe that which was written about him should
receive. The reason is how far you go in life mainly depends on the
spirit within you. Your success in life is fully lied to by what you
believe, every successful person is successful through the leadership
of the spirit behind his or her life. The work Jesus did was successful
through the help of his Father (Spirit God). That's why he said in
John 14:10-11,"Believe thou not that I am in the Father, and the
Father in me? The words that I speak unto you I speak not of
myself: but the Father that dwelled in me, he doeth the works. How
good you can be in business, in marriage, in destiny, in your
profession, and your works are mainly on the spirit pilot-ting your
affairs. To make it work, you must acknowledge him in all your
ways. The writer of Proverbs understood the secret of
acknowledgement to God. Proverbs 3:5-6: Trust in the Lord with all
thy heart, and lean not unto their understanding; In all thy ways
acknowledge him, and he shall direct(organize) your ways. A boy
was possessed by a foul spirit, and from time to time the spirit led
him to destroy his life; until Jesus came and rebuked the spirit; as

the spirit left his life, a new spirit of life entered him and his life shifted to the next level. That was what Jesus revealed to us, whoever believes in him through what the scripture says about him shall receive the Holy Ghost; the spirit which God shall give unto us shall ratify us with powers and might to make exploitation. You must acknowledge God in all your ways to get his attention. Your belief in God prepares you for his blessings. No successful man or woman succeeds without the help of a spirit he/she believes. Your Life and your destiny, your business, and your work could be successful through the association you keep with a spirit you engaged in worship. You might not be good enough at what you are doing because the spirit is not in you (Holy Ghost is a teacher) If the spirit in your life is a good one; once you acknowledge It your life enters the next level. Jesus understood the presence of God in his life and he acknowledged God's work for his ministry to enter the next level on 14:11-14: Believe me that I am in the Father, and the Father in me: or believe me for the very works' sake. Jesus enjoyed the help of God in His life, and He understood that every child of God needs divine help. That's why He the Father to give the company of His spirit. He wants you to unite with him by believing in his ministry so that you could get to your place in Destiny. Verse 12: "Verily, verily, I say unto you, He that believeth on me, the works that I do shall he do also; and greater works than these shall he do; "Your union with God determines how progressive your works will be. The better you acknowledge Him, the faster your answers to your prayers will come. "And whatsoever ye shall ask in my name, that will I do, that the Father may be glorified in the Son. The fact that he has said it, he will do it. Verse 14: If ye shall ask anything in my name, I will do it. This is not a promise but a fact. So one of the ways to make progress in this current time is to believe in him and acknowledge God in everything.

LOCATE THE RIGHT KEYS IN THIS CURRENT TIME.

Psalm 24:7: Lift your heads, O, ye gates; and be ye lifted, ye everlasting doors; and the King of glory shall come in. King of glory is the universal key to success. He is the opener of the door to your next level; everlasting doors open when He comes in. He is strong and mighty, through him all things were

Made.' The fact that the earth remained and the heavens abide; there are invisible doors'. Psalm24:8: Who is this King of glory? The LORD strong and mighty, the LORD in battle. He's the opener of all financial doors, careers, and matrimonial doors. He is the way, the truth, and the life (John14:6). He is the Lord of the host. Psalm24:10: Who is this King of glory? The Lord of hosts, He is the King of glory. All things were made by Him, and without Him was not anything made that was made (John 1:3). He is the Alpha and Omega, the beginning and the ends the first and last (Revelation22:13). It's recommendable that you should know that God is the giver of all right keys that unlocks all doors. The Bible recorded what God said in Isaiah 22:21-22, "And I will clothe him with thy robe, and strengthen him with thy girdle, and I will commit thy government into his hand...; And the key of the house of David will I lay upon his shoulder; so he shall open, and none shall shut, and he shall shut, and none shall open. Each door has its lock, and each lock responds to its right key. When a house is locked, access is denied. Keys are rightly used on a locked house, and every closed house is likely to be unclosed through the right means. The underlined words signify three things that are likely to happen to a building or a house. As much as a building is concerned, regardless of how inestimable the contents of the house are, two things are likely to happen; either the house is locked or is opened. However, what gives you access is the availability of the right key. So when you locate the right key things become accessible to you. Jesus is the ultimate key. We are meant to live a glorious life because the Earth is the Lord and its fullness thereof. Unfortunately, several Christians did not know that the earth is a good place that God has made for mankind, no planet could be better for man except the earth. Genesis 1 to 30, was all about God's creation; but in verse 31 of that chapter (Genesis 1:31), the Bible says, "And God saw everything that he had made, and behold, it was very good...". All that he had made both the heavens and the earth all was very good. That means the earth is a good place for a man to dwell. We are God's people, we belong to him and he has given it in to our hands.

Psalm 24:1: The earth is the Lord, and the fullness thereof; the world, and they that dwell therein. We are not limited to any environmental factor, we are created to rule, we are made victorious. Your Destiny is in your hand, the right key is all you need, discover who you are in God. You are the king's son, and that's who you are in Christ. You have it, God has given it to you through Jesus Christ_ the right key. Prosperity is not for everyone; it is for those who have the right key. The right key is in your hands; all you need to do is to start making use of it. Matthew 16;19: And I will give unto thee the keys of the kingdom of heaven: and whatsoever thou shalt bind on earth shall be bound in heaven: and whatsoever thou shalt loose on earth shall be loosed in heaven. Get up and take the key, Rule your world. The earth is the Campus of God's Word; Loose and take what belongs to you and Let the light shine in your life; Genesis1v3. Every Generation is noted for its blessing. For example, in the Time of old, God blessing people with a long life. Today we are blessed with something glorious. Find out the blessing of your time in next condition of this book so you can get what God has for his people. As student, you need to   know what to do and what you should not do. God said in Jeremiah 33:3, call to me, and I will answer you, and show you a great and mighty thing which you know not. The second edition will teach you additional things you need to know about yourself, your environment, and your right in God. Look for the second edition of this book.

www.ingramcontent.com/pod-product-compliance
Lightning Source LLC
Chambersburg PA
CBHW071942120726
48001CB00005B/2004